– with –

Stampede

visit us at
www.abdopublishing.com

Exclusive Spotlight library bound edition published in 2007 by Spotlight, a division of ABDO Publishing Group, Edina, Minnesota. Spotlight produces high-quality reinforced library bound editions for schools and libraries. Published by agreement with Archie Comic Publications, Inc.

Library of Congress Cataloging-in-Publication Data

Laugh with stampede.
    p. cm. -- (The Archie digest library)
    Revision of issue no. 163 (Feb. 2001) of Laugh digest magazine.
    ISBN-13: 978-1-59961-283-6
    ISBN-10: 1-59961-283-6
    1. Graphic novels. I. Laugh digest magazine. 163. II. Title: Stampede.

PN6728.A72 L47 2007
741.5'973--dc22

                                                        2006051233

All Spotlight books are reinforced library binding
and manufactured in the United States of America.

Contents

A Prince of a Pal! 4

Muddle Huddle 10

Hats Off! 11

Private Eye, Eye 12

Tape Jape 17

Stargazer 18

Draw Drama 29

Talk Balk 30

Tutor Trouble 31

Tune Types 37

Work Shirk 38

Fashion Statement! 39

A Head For Figures 44

A Letter from Antarctica! 45

The Music Man 47

Brain Strain 52

You Take the Cake! 53

Promises to Keep 59

Rain Refrain 80

Laugh

AHEM!! *EXCUSE ME, BUT WHAT ARE YOU DOING GOING THROUGH MR. WEATHERBEE'S FILES?*

WHY ARE YOU *IGNORING* ME? DO I NEED TO CALL IN MR. SVENSON?

Archie & The Gang IN "A PRINCE OF A PAL!"

SCRIPT & PENCILS: BILL GOLLIHER   INKS: RUDY LAPICK
COLORS: BARRY GROSSMAN   LETTERS: BILL YOSHIDA
EDITORS: NELSON RIBEIRO & VICTOR GORELICK   EDITOR-IN-CHIEF: RICHARD GOLDWATER

OH, MS. PHLIPS! HOW ARE YOU?!

MR. WEATHERBEE?! WHAT'S GOING ON? AND WHY ARE YOU *YELLING?!*

I'M SORRY I COULDN'T *HEAR* YOU! I WAS *LISTENING* TO THE LATEST BRANDY SPIRES CD!

WHAT'S WITH ALL *THIS* ANYWAY?

IT'S FROM AN INTERESTING ARTICLE I READ IN PRINCIPAL'S MONTHLY!

"A PRINCIPAL IS A *PRINCE* OF A *PAL*"?

IT TALKS ABOUT HOW A *GOOD* PRINCIPAL SHOULD PUT HIMSELF ON HIS *STUDENT'S LEVEL!*

IF I BECOME ONE OF THEM THEN I CAN UNDERSTAND THEM!

AND THEY CAN UNDERSTAND *ME* BETTER!

NOW IF YOU'LL EXCUSE ME! *SCHOOL'S OUT!*

I'M GOING TO POP'S TO *HANG* WITH MY *PEEPS!*

I PLAN TO FIND *WUZZUP?!*

YOUR TEMPERATURE, I THINK!

PRINCIPAL

HI, GANG! WHAT'S GOING *UP?*

DON'T YOU MEAN "DOWN" MR. WEATHER-BEE?

2

NEXT DAY...

I'M SORRY WE HAD TO DO THAT, MR. WEATHERBEE!

IT'S ALL RIGHT! I NEEDED SOMETHING TO SNAP ME BACK TO *REALITY!*

I REALIZE NOW I CAN BE MORE UNDERSTANDING OF THE KIDS WITHOUT MAKING A *FOOL* OF MYSELF!

MR. WEATHERBEE, SUPERINTENDENT HASSEL IS HERE TO SEE YOU!

OH, SEND HIM IT!

WEATHERBEE, *WUZZUP?* I WANTED TO SHARE THIS GREAT ARTICLE I READ IN *PRINCIPAL'S MONTHLY* WITH YOU!

PRINCIPAL'S MONTHLY

IT SAYS YOU'VE GOT TO CHILL WITH YOUR CREW!

YOU KNOW, GET THE *4-1-1* ON WHAT'S *GOING DOWN...* BLAH... BLAH... BLAH...

SOMETHING TELLS ME YOU GUYS BETTER GET THE *SCOOTER* READY AGAIN!

PRINCIPAL

THE END

Veronica HATS OFF!

SEE HOW MANY DIFFERENT HATS YOU
CAN FIND IN THIS PUZZLE!

L	N	Q	S	Y	B	R	E	D	
Z	A	X	B	E	Z	E	W	K	
V	G	C	R	M	I	F	O	Y	
P	K	E	Y	N	Z	U	R	X	
E	T	T	A	H	P	O	T	C	
T	V	E	R						
J	B	D	O						
A	G	F	D						
C	A	P	E						
H	I	B	F						

WORD LIST — FEDORA,
TOP HAT, DERBY, BEANIE,
BERET, CAP

GOOD GRIEF! THE BOY IS HYSTERICAL WITH AMUSEMENT!

WHOOPS! HYA HAHA HOO!

YUK YUK!

WHAT'S SO FUNNY, REGGIE?

OMIGOSH! HE THINKS HE'S MICKEY SQUILLANE!!

HEE HEE!

...OR-AGATHA CRISPY!

IT'S UNUSUAL TO HEAR GALES OF LAUGHTER IN THE SCHOOL HALLS! DON'T KEEP IT ALL TO YOURSELF!

H-HEAR THIS, MR. WEATHERBEE!

HYOK!

HEE HEE HEE!

OH, MY STARS!! THIS IS HILARIOUS!!

ER-EXCUSE ME! IS THAT MY LOST RECORDER?

HA! I CAN'T WAIT TO HEAR THE END OF THIS LAUGH RIOT!

F-FUNNY!! JUGGIE, YOU'RE A GREAT COMEDY WRITER!!

HMPH! SOME PEOPLE WOULDN'T KNOW TALENT IF IT JUMPED UP AND BIT THEM!

SHUGHEAD, VOULD YOU HELP OL' SVENSON BY CLEANING DE OLD FILES FROM DIS CABINET ZO I CAN MOVE IT INTO DE BASEMENT?

SURE, SVEN! AT LEAST *YOU'RE* NOT LAUGHING!

MAN! THIS IS OLD, OLD STUFF! THE BEE SHOULD HAVE CLEANED IT OUT YEARS AGO!

OKAY! THAT'S THE END OF THOSE DUSTY OLD FILES! NOTHING IN THIS DRAWER NOW, BUT--BUT--?

-- AN OLD COLLEGE RING! NOW, WHO?.... HEY, IT'S GOT *INITIALS* IN IT!!

PRINCIP

ER-MR. WEATHERBEE! YOU FOUND MY PORTRAYAL OF A DETECTIVE TO BE *FUNNY*?

HEE, HEE! UNBELIEVABLY FUNNY, SON!

YOU-UH-*DID* GO TO *COLLEGE*, DIDN'T YOU, SIR?

DID YOU EXPECT YOUR PRINCIPAL TO BE A DROP-OUT? *OF COURSE* I WENT TO COLLEGE.!!

4

Archie -in- "TAPE JAPE"

DAD! I MADE A *SPECIAL TAPE!* ON OUR HOME VIDEO RECORDER!

I WANT YOU TO WATCH IT!

THE FOLLOWING FACTS WILL EXPLAIN WHY I DESPERATELY NEED AN ALLOWANCE INCREASE!

I'M EVEN GETTING *COMMERCIALS* FROM MY OWN FAMILY!

END

BETTY and Veronica IN "STARGAZER"

PART ONE

THIS CLASSY COLA IS A REAL THIRST-QUENCHER, RON!

YOU SOUND LIKE A PRODUCT ENDORSEMENT FOR MY FATHER'S NEW SODA COMPANY, BETTY!

MUSIC TV

I'D BE HAPPY TO HELP YOUR FATHER SELL THIS STUFF! IT TASTES GREAT!

UNFORTUNATELY NO ONE ELSE SEEMS TO KNOW THAT! THE SALES OF CLASSY COLA ARE FIZZING!

LOOK! IT'S AMERICA'S ULTIMATE BABE BLONDONNA!

SHE'S EVERY GUY'S DREAMY DATE, INCLUDING ARCHIE'S!

ARCHIE THINKS SHE'S IRRESISTIBLE! THEY SAY SHE'S DATED OVER 100 HOLLYWOOD HUNKS!

- AND BROKEN EVERY ONE OF THEIR HEARTS!

ARCHIE DOESN'T EVEN CARE THAT SHE HAS A REPUTATION FOR *LOVING* AND *LEAVING*!

WELL, I LOVE THE CLOTHES SHE WEARS!

MAYBE WE COULD DO A PROMOTION WHERE A LUCKY GUY WINS A DATE WITH HER!

IT SOUNDS LIKE DADDYKINS HAS COMPANY!

EEK! IT'S *HER!* HER! HER!!

WHO?

WHO?

WHO?

EEK!

STOP ACTING LIKE AN OWL, BETTY! *BLONDONNA,* THAT'S WHO!

CLASSY LOLA

2

NOT REALLY, RON! IN FACT IF YOU AND BETTY COULD TAKE ME SHOPPING WHERE NO ONE WOULD RECOGNIZE ME, I'D APPRECIATE IT!

SURE! RIVERDALE MALL IS ALWAYS SO CROWDED, YOU'LL BLEND RIGHT IN!

GREAT! LET'S GO TOMORROW! IS IT OKAY IF I USE THE PHONE FOR A PERSONAL CALL?

OF COURSE! USE THE ONE IN THE NEXT ROOM!

NEXT DAY AT THE MALL...

THANKS FOR LENDING ME SOME OF YOUR CLOTHES, RON! DO I LOOK ORDINARY ENOUGH?

YOU LOOK JUST LIKE RON, A PERFECT NOBODY!

HEY!

I MEAN ... NO ONE WOULD RECOGNIZE HER AS A FAMOUS ROCK STAR!

HUMPH! BETTY'S RIGHT!

NO ONE WILL EVEN NOTICE YOU HERE!

SUPER! IT FEELS GOOD TO WEAR COMFORTABLE CLOTHES LIKE THIS FOR A CHANGE!

4

I DON'T SEE THEM ANYWHERE!

THEY'RE GONE!

MUSIC

GGH! I HOPE EVERYTHING WILL BE OKAY! THAT GUY LOOKED SUSPICIOUS!

YEAH! SUSPICIOUS, BUT ALSO FAMILIAR! I THINK I'VE SEEN HIM BEFORE, BUT I CAN'T REMEMBER WHERE!

LATER:

JEANZ

HI, GIRLS! I HAD A GREAT TIME! WE CAN LEAVE NOW!

BLONDONNA! IT'S LATE! WE WERE WORRIED!

LUNCH LOUNGE

HMMM! IF SHE WAS SHOPPING, WHERE ARE HER PACKAGES?

WORRIED ABOUT WHAT?

WE SAW A STRANGE GUY FOLLOWING YOU!

GUY?

WHAT GUY?

END PART 1

Star-Gazer PART TWO

DADDYKINS, I'M WORRIED ABOUT BLONDONNA!

QUITE HONESTLY, SO AM I! I'VE BEEN THINKING ABOUT OUR DEAL DURING THE FEW DAYS SHE'S BEEN HERE!

WE'RE PAYING HER A LOT OF MONEY, AND I'M NOT SURE HER WILD IMAGE IS THE RIGHT WAY TO SELL CLASSY COLA!

BLONDONNA NASTY GAL #5

WHAT DO YOU MEAN?

I WANT CLASSY COLA TO BE A REFRESHING DRINK FOR THE ENTIRE FAMILY, NOT JUST A FAD DRINK FOR YOUNG FUN SEEKERS!

7

EXCUSE ME! IS IT ALL RIGHT IF I TAKE A STROLL AROUND THE ESTATE?

CERTAINLY, ENJOY YOUR MOONLIGHT WALK!

BLONDONNA REALLY ISN'T LIKE HER IMAGE! I THINK SHE'S THE PERFECT PERSON TO SELL CLASSY COLA!

WELL I HOPE SO!

QUICK, RON! COME HERE!

WHAT IS IT, BETTY?

LOOK! IT'S THAT GUY AGAIN!

OH NO! HE MUST HAVE FOLLOWED BLONDONNA HERE SOMEHOW!

I'LL TELL DADDYKINS TO GET SMITHERS TO ALERT THE POLICE!

HURRY, RON! I SEE THEM! HE'S SNEAKING UP BEHIND HER!

Archie in "TUTOR TROUBLE"

I'VE GOT AN IDEA! I NEED CHEMISTRY HELP AND YOU NEED GIRL HELP, WHY DON'T WE *TUTOR* EACH OTHER?

THAT'S GREAT! WE CAN GET STARTED TONIGHT AT MY HOUSE!

AND SO.... THE BASIS OF CHEMISTRY IS THE PERIODIC TABLE OF THE ELEMENTS! YOU NEED TO *LEARN* THEM AND THEIR *SYMBOLS!*

HOW CAN I *REMEMBER* ALL THIS? IT LOOKS SO *BORING!*

SIMPLY FIND A WAY TO MAKE IT *INTERESTING* TO YOU!

YOU KNOW GIRLS APPRECIATE A GOOD MEMORY, TOO! THE *MORE* INFORMATION YOU CAN REMEMBER ABOUT THEM THE *BETTER!*

REALLY?

LATER... DILTON SAID COME UP WITH A WAY TO MAKE THIS INTERESTING!

HOW ABOUT ALL THE *ELEMENTS* ARE BEAUTIFUL GIRLS WITH *SYMBOLS* ON THEIR *T-SHIRTS!*

2

I'M MAGNESIUM!

HI! I'M NEON!

(SIGH!) YEP! THIS COULD WORK!

MEANWHILE... THERE! I'VE STUDIED THE YEAR-BOOK AND MEMORIZED THE NAMES OF ALL THE GIRLS IN SCHOOL AND A LITTLE INFO ON EACH!...THEY SHOULD BE IMPRESSED!

RIVERDALE HIGH 2000

AND SO... ARCHIE, ABOUT THE POP QUIZ ON THE TABLE OF ELEMENTS...

YES, SIR! HOW'D I DO, PROF. FLUTESNOOT?

LAB

PRETTY WELL, BUT FOR MAGNESIUM INSTEAD OF LISTING THE SYMBOL, YOU WROTE...

...THE HOT BLONDE WITH BLUE EYES AND THE LEGS THAT WON'T QUIT!

ULP!

AND... HI, LISA JENKINS! I'M DILTON DOILEY!

HI! DO I KNOW YOU?

3

AND SO... THERE! I'VE ACQUIRED THE *E-MAIL* ADDRESSES OF *ALL* THE GIRLS IN SCHOOL AND *SEPARATED* OUT ALL THE ONES WHO HAVE *BOY-FRIENDS*!

NOW TO SEND A *ROMANTIC LITTLE LOVE NOTE* TO ALL THE OTHERS!

YOUR MAIL HAS BEEN SENT!

NEXT DAY...

DUH, DILTON, I THOUGHT WE WERE FRIENDS!

WE ARE, MOOSE! WHAT ARE YOU TALKING ABOUT?

YOU SENT MY GIRL, *MIDGE*, THIS LOVEY-DOVEY *E-MAIL*!

EEP!

WINK

OH, NO! I SENT MY NOTE TO ALL THE GIRLS WITH *BOYFRIENDS* BY MISTAKE!

THERE *HE* IS!

MEANWHILE...

DILTON SAID TO PAY CLOSE ATTENTION! I'LL MAKE SURE TO PUT IN THE EXACT NUMBER OF DROPS!

1-2-3...

HERE I AM ... SINGING AGAIN! DISCOVER WHAT KINDS OF TUNES I LIKE TO BELT OUT BY FINDING THE MUSIC TYPES IN THE WORD SEARCH! LOOK UP, DOWN, FORWARDS, BACKWARDS, AND DIAGONALLY! CROSS THEM OFF AS YOU FIND THEM! RING-A-DING-DING! ♫

TUNE TYPES:
BALLAD
TORCH
COUNTRY
ROCK
POP
SWING
JAZZ
BOP
RAP

Jughead — "WORK SHIRK"

THAT SNOW IS REALLY COMING DOWN!

CLASS, YOU CAN ALL LEAVE FOR HOME IF YOU WANT TO!

AaBbCcDdEeFfGg

HISTORY PAGES 78-9/06

JUGHEAD, I SAID YOU COULD GO HOME!

I'M IN NO HURRY TO GET HOME, MISS GRUNDY!

--- MY DAD IS SHOVELLING THE SIDEWALK!

END

UH-OH! IT'S DELLA THE HEAD WITCH!

OF COURSE! WHO ELSE MAKES THOSE KIND OF ENTRANCES!?

SO, SABRINA, YOU DON'T THINK THE OTHER WITCHES' OUTFITS ARE GOOD ENOUGH FOR YOU!

YOU DON'T WEAR THEM!

BEING HEAD WITCH HAS ITS PRIVILEGES!

NOW PUT ON THIS OUTFIT BEFORE I REVOKE YOUR POWERS!

OKAY! BUT THIS IS GOING TO BE EMBARRASSING!

POOF!

AND SO...

MR. KLINE! WHAT DOES IT TAKE TO POPULARIZE A LOOK?

OH, I CAN MAKE ANY LOOK POPULAR!

APPEARING TODAY
KELVIN KLINE
★
DESIGNER

WHATEVER THE NEXT PERSON TO COME AROUND THE CORNER IS WEARING, I'LL BET I COULD TURN INTO THE NEXT RAGE!

Bloomin Dales

THE
GYP
B

2

UH-OH! IT LOOKS LIKE YOU COULD HAVE YOUR WORK CUT OUT FOR YOU!

EEP!

; SIGH ;

NO, I SAID I'LL DO IT, AND I *WILL*!

HELLO, YOUNG LADY! I'M KELVIN KLINE THE DESIGNER! MAY I SPEAK WITH YOU?!

SURE!

AND IN A FEW MONTHS...

I PRESENT MY NEW *WITCH LOOK*, INSPIRED BY MY FRIEND SABRINA!

HE... EXPECTS US TO WEAR *THAT?!*

KELVIN KLINE

AND SO...

WOW! A BILLBOARD IN *TIMES SQUARE*... THIS IS THE GREATEST!

Kelvin Kline

TICKETS

K-Kola

SUN FILM

③

The END.

Moose in "BRAIN STRAIN"

$X^3 + 2AB$

OH, BOY! DESE MATH PROBLEMS HURT MY HEAD!

D-UH, MISS GRUNDY, MAY I LEAVE EARLY FOR FOOTBALL PRACTICE?

YES, MOOSE, YOU MAY!

ALL RIGHT, GUYS! I HAVE SOME PLAYS I WANT YOU TO MEMORIZE!

COACH

IN THIS PITCH-OUT THAT STARTS FROM THE SPLIT-T, THE BALL GOES TO THE RIGHT HALFBACK!

COACH

--- HE THEN FAKES A HAND-OFF TO THE FULLBACK, WHILE CRISS-CROSSING WITH THE QUARTERBACK, WHO CUTS BACK---

D-UH, MISS GRUNDY, MAY I COME BACK IN?

?

END

AN AFTERNOON MOVIE SOUNDS GREAT! THE GUYS AREN'T PAYING ATTENTION TO *ME* ANYWAY!

MEET YOU AT THE MULTIPLEX IN A FEW! 'BYE!

GUYS! I'M GOING TO A MOVIE WITH VERONICA. I'LL BE BACK IN A *COUPLE OF HOURS!*

SURE!

WHERE ARE YOU GOING?!

TO CHECK OUT THE KITCHEN, OF COURSE!

THAT *CAKE* LOOKS *GREAT!*

BETTY HAD IT OUT ON THE COUNTER SO I ASSUMED IT WAS FAIR GAME!

I'LL GET A *SLICE,* TOO!

GREAT! I'VE GOT TO HAVE *SOME MORE!*

SOON... UH-OH! WE ATE THE *WHOLE THING!*

IT COULDN'T BE HELPED! IT WAS *TOO TASTY!*

WHAT'S THIS?! AN ENTRY FORM FOR THE RIVERDALE *BAKE-OFF!*

BAKE-OFF!

OH, NO! I WAS ONLY *HALFWAY* PAYING ATTENTION, BUT I HEARD BETTY TELLING VERONICA THAT SHE HAD *BAKED* SOMETHING FOR TONIGHT'S BAKE-OFF!

OOPS!

BURP!

WHAT'LL WE DO? WE SPOILED HER CHANCES!

SIMPLE! WE'VE GOT TIME! WE'LL MAKE THE *EXACT SAME CAKE!*

THE RECIPE BOOK IS STILL OPENED TO THAT PAGE!

WE'LL MISS PART OF THE GAME, BUT WE'VE GOT TO DO WHAT WE HAVE TO DO!

SOON... THAT SHOULD DO IT!

PUT IT IN THE OVEN AT 300° FOR FIFTY MINUTES!

NOW! LET'S GO GET BACK TO THE *GAME!*

3

WELL, I'M GOING TO MAKE A NEW YEAR'S RESOLUTION ANYWAY!

HMMM! NOW WHAT BAD HABIT DO I NEED TO RID MYSELF OF?

(GASP!) OF COURSE! IT'S SO OBVIOUS!!

THE NASTY WAY I HAVE OF ALWAYS TRYING TO COME BETWEEN ARCHIE AND VERONICA!!

IT'S MY FAVORITE PASTIME AND IT WILL BE A PAINFUL HABIT TO BREAK, BUT...

THE WHOLE IDEA OF RESOLUTIONS IS TO STRENGTHEN YOUR CHARACTER! BY GEORGE, I CAN BE AS STRONG AS THE NEXT JEALOUS FEMALE!

3

NEXT DAY!

RON! I'VE *GOT* IT! I HAVE DECIDED ON MY NEW YEAR'S RESOLUTION.!!

WELL, BULLY FOR YOU! WHAT *IS* IT?

I *CAN'T* TELL YOU.! TO REVEAL IT WOULD WEAKEN MY RESOLVE.! BUT IT WILL MAKE ME A BETTER PERSON.!

BUT, I'M YOUR BEST FRIEND.!

SURELY YOU CAN TELL ME.!

SORRY, RON.! MY LIPS ARE SEALED.!

HUMPH.! SHE *KNOWS* I CAN'T STAND BEING LEFT OUT OF SOMETHING.!!

SMARMY, SELF-SATISFIED, YELLOWHAIRED YAHOO.! HOW CAN I MAKE HER BREAK HER RESOLUTION IF I DON'T KNOW WHAT IT IS?

HOLY COW.! WHEN SHE STARTS SNARLING TO HERSELF IT'S TIME TO STAY OUT OF SIGHT.!

④

- *BUT SOME MOODS CAN CHANGE VERY QUICKLY!*...

I'VE SEEN THAT GRIN BEFORE, DEAR! YOU LOOK LIKE A CAT WHO SWALLOWED THE CANARY!

I'M A HAPPY CAMPER, DADDY!

I DECIDED ON MY NEW YEAR'S RESOLUTION!

YOU? MS. PERFECTION! *YOU'RE* MAKING A RESOLUTION?

MY RESOLUTION IS TO MAKE BETTY BREAK *HERS*...WHATEVER IT *IS!*

NOW, NOW, DEAR! THAT'S NOT VERY NICE, IS IT?

DEAR, SWEET DADDY! "NICE" IS FOR OTHERS... NOT FOR *ME!*

WHERE DID I GO WRONG?

... AND, AGAIN... SHE'S GOT *RADAR!* SHE ALWAYS KNOWS WHEN WE'RE TOGETHER! WATCH HER HORN IN ON OUR DATE!

I *KNEW* IT!

YOU MEAN YOUR BEST FRIEND?

LOOK! SHE'S GOING THE OTHER WAY! NOW AREN'T YOU ASHAMED OF YOUR SUSPICIONS?

EEP! I CAN'T BELIEVE IT!

END OF PART ONE

I THINK I CAN-- I THINK I CAN... I THINK I CAN... I *KNOW* I CAN...

(SIGH) THAT'S WHY NEW YEAR'S RESOLUTIONS ARE SO OFTEN FAILURES!

YOU LOOK PLEASED WITH YOURSELF! WHAT'S UP?

I HAVE RESOLVED *NOT* TO INTERFERE WITH RONNIE'S LOVE LIFE!

I THOUGHT YOU HAD MORE SENSE, BETTY!

YOU DON'T THINK I CAN *DO* IT?

NOBODY KEEPS A NEW YEAR'S RESOLUTION! IT'S THE WAY OF THE WORLD!

I'LL KEEP *THIS* ONE! I'M STRONG WILLED!

TROUBLE IS, PEOPLE ALWAYS RESOLVE TO GIVE UP SOMETHING THEY REALLY *ENJOY* DOING!

OF COURSE!

THAT'S WHY THEY ALWAYS GET BROKEN! YOU'VE GOTTA DO WHAT I DO!

AND WHAT'S THAT?

②

WELL, MY RESOLUTION THIS YEAR WILL BE TO GIVE UP *DIETING!*

BUT, JUGGIE! *YOU* NEVER DIET!

RIGHT! THAT'S WHY I'LL SUCCEED WHILE ALL OTHERS FAIL!

JUGHEAD JONES! THAT'S UTTERLY RIDICULOUS!

I DON'T NEED TO FIND AN EASY WAY OUT! I CAN HANDLE THIS RESOLUTION BUSINESS THE RIGHT WAY!

US MAIL

EEP!

THERE THEY ARE AGAIN...! NOW, GIRL, THIS IS NO TIME TO WEAKEN!

ALL IT TAKES IS A STRONG WILL AND DETERMINATION!

LOOK, ARCHIE! THERE SHE GOES AGAIN! DELIBERATELY AVOIDING US!

HMMM! I GOTTA ADMIT, THAT'S PRETTY UNUSUAL!

3

RON! SHE MADE IT CLEAR THAT SHE DOESN'T WANT TO SEE US!

OH, HUSH UP, ARCHIE!

W-W-WHAT ARE YOU TWO DOING HERE?

WE'RE GOING TO A MOVIE AND DECIDED TO INVITE YOU!

ER-N-NO THANKS, RON! I HAVE SOMETHING TO DO!

NONSENSE! YOU'RE COMING WITH US! YOU'LL *LOVE* THIS FILM!

DRAG — SCRAPE

RON! I CAN'T SIT BETWEEN YOU AND ARCHIE! AFTER ALL, IT'S *YOUR* DATE!!

DON'T ARGUE, BETTY! NOTHING'S TOO GOOD FOR MY BEST FRIEND!

HAH! I DON'T KNOW *WHAT* HER IDIOTIC RESOLUTION WAS, BUT I'M PRETTY SURE I'VE DEEPSIXED IT SOMEHOW!

(SIGH) JUGGIE WAS RIGHT! RESOLUTIONS ARE IMPOSSIBLE TO KEEP! AH, WELL, YOU WIN SOME, YOU LOSE SOME!

END OF PART TWO

PROMISES TO KEEP
PART III

SAW YOU AT THE MOVIES YESTERDAY, BETTY! THAT RESOLUTION DIDN'T LAST VERY LONG, DID IT?

YOU WERE *SO* RIGHT, JUGGIE! I GUESS I'M JUST AS WEAK-WILLED AS I AM *HAPPY* ABOUT IT!

THE NEW YEAR ALWAYS BRINGS OUT WEIRD THINGS IN PEOPLE!

DID I JUST HEAR JUGHEAD JONES DEFINING *OTHER PEOPLE* AS *WEIRD?*

WHEN IT COMES TO RESOLUTIONS-- *YES SIR!*

THEY NEVER LEARN! THEY ALWAYS MAKE RESOLUTIONS THEY *CAN'T* KEEP!

THAT'S NONSENSE, SON!

WHEN AN *ADULT* RESOLVES TO DO SOMETHING ... HE FOLLOWS THROUGH!

W-ELL, I SUPPOSE *SOME* PEOPLE, LIKE *SCHOOL PRINCIPALS*, ARE MORE EXCEPTIONAL THAN OTHERS!

HMMM! THAT BOY SPREADS OIL LIKE A LEAKY TANKER!

OH, CHIEF! A WORD WITH YOU IF YOU HAVE TIME!

DO YOU REALIZE THE NEW YEAR IS ALMOST UPON US?

YES, GERALDINE! HAVE YOU MADE ANY RESOLUTIONS YET?

I'VE NEVER BEEN SO SUCCESSFUL IN *KEEPING* THEM, BOSS!

WELL, I GUESS I'M MADE OF STERNER STUFF!

IT'S JUST A MATTER OF WILL POWER AND DETERMINATION!

WOULD YOU CARE TO GIVE ME AN EXAMPLE?

2

END OF PART THREE